The Ho

A Chough's Tale

A book from
The Manor House Stories

written and illustrated by
Jani Tully Chaplin

This book belongs to

....

Printed in the UK by Cambrian Printers
Typesetting and design by JS Typesetting Ltd, Porthcawl, Mid Glamorgan

FSC
www.fsc.org
MIX
Paper from
responsible sources
FSC® C005094

Last night I dreamt I went to Cornwall again …

In his bedroom at the top of the Manor House, Chesterfield Penguin the Butler awoke from his dream of sand dunes, salty air, white surf, windswept tamarisk bushes, ice cream and pasties. Listening to the sound of the sea in one of his shells, he quickly made up his mind.

"Time to take the youngsters on holiday!" he declared. Miranda Mistlethrush and the Willow Tit twins, Arthur and Sebastian, would be so excited.

Someone else in the bedroom overheard Chesterfield; it was one of the Manor House Mice who lived behind the skirting board.

"Whoopee! A holiday!" squeaked Marzipan Mouse.

Rory Redshank the Footman moved the caravan out of the coach house, dusted it off and brought it to the front of the Manor House.

Delia Duck the Cook filled its lockers with tasty provisions, while Sarah Sparrow the Scullery Maid brought freshly laundered bedlinen and towels from the airing cupboard.

At last everything was ready.

There was just enough room at the back of the caravan for Miranda, Arthur and Sebastian; even the Manor House Mice found a tiny corner for their luggage. They always wanted to join in.

Soon the caravan was trundling along the country lanes, the little Dartmoor pony's hooves clip-clopping in time to the rattling pots and pans hanging on their hooks.

Once across the River Tamar, the stone hedges sparkled with flowers; tall foxgloves swayed against a clear blue sky and the air was filled with a scent of coconut from the yellow gorse blossom.

"When will we get there?" asked Arthur.

"Not quite yet," answered Chesterfield.

"Aren't we there YET?" demanded Sebastian, who always copied his brother.

"Why don't you play a game?" Rory suggested. "When I used to go to Cornwall with my parents we always counted the names on signposts beginning with TRE. We used to lose count before we reached Bodmin! By the TRE, the POL and the PEN, shall you know your Cornishmen. That's how the rhyme goes."

"Ooh good!" said Arthur to Sebastian. "You can count the TRE-s, I'll take the POL-s and Miranda can have the PEN-s."

Meanwhile high on a Cornish clifftop, his feathers gently ruffled by the salty Atlantic breeze, sat a handsome young chough.

Charles Pencarrow Poldrake Treyarnon Chough had always wanted to help look after the steam engine at the tin mine, just like his father and grandfather before him.

But this young chough could not even look after himself, because he had never learnt to fly.

Giving a little shudder as he gazed out to sea, he remembered the fateful day of his accident when he was still a tiny choughling.

He had hatched out of his egg one warm day in early summer. His cosy nest, comfortably lined with sheep's wool and horse hair, was tucked into a crevice on the cliff.

A fresh breeze whipped the waves far below, tousling the sea pinks so they looked like dancing ladies wearing sugar-pink bath hats.

"Your family names are very ancient, just like me!" his grandmother had told him when he was born.

"But they are far too long for me," she explained. "So I will call you Chuff instead; after all, 'Chuff' is the only sound you can make at the moment. You will only earn your full name when you have learnt to fly."

"Chee-ow!" was the call of the grown-up choughs, but Chuff could not yet manage this.

"Yow, Chuff," they greeted him cheerily as they swept past, their bright red beaks glinting in the sun. "Soon you'll be flying just like us!"

Now choughs are famous for being acrobats of the air, swooping and diving like aerial daredevils in the updrafts beside the Cornish cliffs.

"Will I ever be able to fly like them?" he asked himself doubtfully.

"Never stray near the cliff edge until you have learnt to fly," his mother had often warned him. But of course Chuff thought he knew best.

Early one morning he had peered over the clifftop to see for himself just how far it was to the sharp rocks and sea below.

Suddenly a gust of wind caught Chuff from behind, toppling him straight over the edge. Down he tumbled head over heels like a black powderpuff.

Hard as he tried, his little wings simply would not work.

Over and over he went, falling faster and faster. His tummy churned as the jagged black rocks came closer and closer.

"HELP, H-E-L-P!" he screeched, but his cries were carried away by the wind.

Luckily for Chuff, an enormous herring gull happened to be gliding past and spotted the falling choughling.

He swooped gracefully underneath Chuff and caught him, cradling him gently between his broad, outstretched wings.

"Oh thank you, Mr. Gull," panted Chuff, very out of breath and trembling with fright.

"Don't mention it young 'un," replied the gull. "Lucky I was passing just as you began your skydive!"

"I didn't mean to fall off the cliff," said Chuff shakily. "I'm Charles Pencarrow Poldrake Treyarnon Chough, but you can call me Chuff for short," said the little choughling.

"Well good morning, Chuff. I'm the Coastguard, Sailor Oswald Seagull. You can call me SOS for short," the gull replied with a wink.

"And what do you want to be when you grow up?" enquired Sailor Oswald.

"I want to watch over the steam engine at the tin mine, so I can have a pasty for my lunch just like the miners." Chuff answered.

Now, as you will understand, choughs do not really eat pasties, but Chuff did not know this.

He only knew that pasties smelt delicious and that the miners held onto the crust while they ate the rest of the pasty, throwing it away when they had finished.

"Well I must be off to catch some silver darlings, as we seabirds call them, for my lunch. It's been nice meeting you, Chuff."

"Take care now, you choughs are rare enough already!" called Oswald as he flew off towards the herring shoals, which had been spotted further out at sea.

Two years had passed since that day when Sailor Oswald Seagull had rescued Chuff, but he had never plucked up enough courage to fly. He shook himself, trying to forget his accident.

At that moment Chuff spotted a splendid caravan next to the track beside the beach. Slowly he began to hop and flap his way down the path towards it, hoping to find some new friends.

Arthur and Sebastian had gone to the beach, searching for shells and small pieces of coloured glass, washed smooth by the sand and sea, to add to their collection.

Miranda was picking wild flowers on a grassy mound above the track, where she was surprised by the arrival of an unusual visitor; she had never seen a bird like Chuff before.

With his glossy black feathers and long, bright red beak that matched his legs, Miranda thought he was very handsome.

"Good morning," she said. "My brothers and I arrived here last night for a holiday."

"Welcome to Cornwall," he replied quietly. "I'm Chuff. I live up there, on the cliffs."

Miranda thought he looked very unhappy.

"It must be very dangerous being so high up. Don't you ever get frightened?" asked Miranda, as Chuff hung his head in shame and stared at the ground.

"Why are you so sad?" asked Miranda, who had a soft heart and always wanted to help.

"I am too scared to fly," replied Chuff. "You see, I had an accident when I was very young and now Mother says I can only help at the tin mine when I have learnt to fly."

Miranda thought for a minute before producing a red and white spotty scarf, which had been used for carrying her picnic.

"This is a magic scarf," she said. "With this around your neck you will be able to fly beautifully!"

"And never forget," she added, "you can do absolutely anything you want to do, if you set your mind to it."

At that moment, Arthur and Sebastian came back from the beach, eager to meet Miranda's new friend. Miranda explained to them all about Chuff's fear of flying.

"Don't worry, Chuff, look at us!" called the twins as they took off and fluttered above Chuff's head. "Flying is easy!"

Chuff was delighted and filled with fresh hope. Encouraged by Miranda and the twins, with the scarf tied firmly around his neck, he ran as fast as his thin red legs could carry him.

Faster and faster he went, skimming across the ground until his feet hardly touched the grass. Suddenly he felt the draught beneath his wings and rose up, up into the air. He was FLYING!

"Hurrah! Hurrah!" cried Miranda, Arthur and Sebastian.

Chuff couldn't believe it, he was soaring, swooping, diving and floating just like every other chough. He flew on and on, higher and higher still, until he saw the tin mine far below.

It seemed to Chuff that the scarf was very magical indeed.

"I'll go and visit the engine house," Chuff thought to himself.

Swooping down to the mine, he tried to turn sharply towards the entrance. Too sharply!

He wobbled this way and that, lost his balance and fell head over heels until PLOP! He was inside something and it was very dark.

Chuff had fallen straight down the tall chimney stack of the engine house.

With a thump he landed on a small ledge halfway down the chimney. Luckily for Chuff, the engine was not working, although the sooty ledge was still warm.

Blinking in the darkness he shook his feathers and wondered how he was ever going to get out again. He could see daylight at the top of the stack, but it was such a long way up and he knew he could not take off from the ledge.

Miranda and the twins had seen Chuff disappearing into the stack and quickly flew back to ask Rory Redshank for help.

Within a few minutes Rory Redshank was darting towards the mine with a coil of sturdy rope borrowed from the caravan.

He flew to the top of the chimney stack and landed very carefully on the rim.

"Don't panic, young fella; I will get you out," Rory called. "Just keep very still!"

Rory leant over into the stack and held tightly to the edge. He lowered the rope down the stack until Chuff could take hold. Rory pulled gently until the young Chough appeared at the top.

As they sat on top of the stack to catch their breath, Rory asked Chuff why he wanted to help at the mine.

"I just can't resist anything shiny," said Chuff. Like all magpies and jackdaws, choughs love to collect any glittering objects. Often they borrow them to decorate their nests.

"There are all sorts of interesting brass dials and levers in the engine house, and plenty of screws and washers lying around too," added Chuff, flying down to admire the steam engine through the window. "Father often brings shiny bits and pieces home for Mother."

Chuff flew confidently back to the caravan with Rory, where the others were waiting anxiously.

"Thank you so much for rescuing me," said Chuff, who had made a perfect landing beside them. "I will never be afraid to fly any more."

"You just need to practise those turns," said Rory kindly.

"Goodbye my dear friends," said Chuff. "Enjoy the rest of your holiday, I hope I shall see you all again next summer."

The time flew by with sun filled-days and star-filled nights, but like all good things the holiday soon came to its end.

"All aboard!" called Chesterfield from the caravan.

It was time to leave Cornwall and head home to the Manor House. In the distance the Ding Dong Bell chimed, as if to say farewell to the little party.

"Home, James and don't spare the horses!" joked Rory.

"But Chesterfield is driving, not James," said Arthur.

"And we only have a pony, not horses!" added Sebastian.

"It's just an old saying," explained Rory.

But the twins were not really listening as they settled into their bunks in the caravan, busily examining their new found seashells.

"When we get home tomorrow, you could both make shell boxes to keep your treasures safe," suggested Miranda, as the caravan trundled and rattled steadily up the track on its long journey home to the Manor House.

Back on the clifftop Chuff told his mother about his adventure.

"Now I can fly you will let me help with the steam engine at the mine, won't you?" he asked.

"Of course, dear," said his mother. "I always knew you could do it. After all you are Charles Pencarrow Poldrake Treyarnon Chough."

Chuff sighed happily, watching the sky turn red as the sun set.

... and the scent of pasties blew towards him with the salt wind from the sea.

THE END

How to make a shell box

You will need a small wooden, or stiff cardboard box with a lid, a selection of seashells, some child-safe PVA white glue and a small paintbrush you don't want to use again!

Cover the table you are using with newspaper. Practice arranging the shells on the lid of your box until you like the design. Lift them off and put to one side carefully in the same pattern. Spread glue evenly onto the lid and sides with the brush, one face at a time, and press the shells gently but firmly into position. Leave overnight to dry.

To bring out the colours, ask an adult to spray the box with clear varnish.

The Chough – a proud emblem of Cornwall

Choughs were once a common sight in Cornwall; but by the end of the 19th century, at the same time as the 2,500 year-old Cornish tin and copper mining industry was facing its end, they were already disappearing fast. As the miners and their grazing livestock moved from the land above the cliffs of western Cornwall, so the pasture slowly vanished. The ground became overgrown and the choughs could no longer find their diet of insects, ants and beetles. Persecution by farmers and Victorian collectors hastened this sad decline.

Today there are seven pairs of choughs in the wild in Cornwall, thanks largely to the efforts of the Cornwall Chough Conservation Network, (CCCN), to which the author voluntarily contributes from sales of this book. The CCCN is a group of organisations and individuals including the RSPB, The National Trust and Natural England.

Did you know?

The collective name for choughs is a Clattering of Choughs.

Legend has it that the spirit of King Arthur returned to Cornwall as a chough.

The old Cornish name for chough is palores, which means 'digger', after the way they find their food.

The deepest Cornish tin mine shaft, at Dolcoath, is 3,300 feet (1,000 m) deep.

Tunnels and shafts at the Levant mine extend 1½ miles (2½ km) out to sea.

A geranium was always grown on the windowsill of Cornish mine engine houses.

The Ding Dong Bell, now on display by the font at Madron Church, was rung daily to mark the last shift at the Ding Dong Mines on the Land's End Peninsula.

Richard Trevithic, a Cornishman and mine engineer, demonstrated the world's first steam engine powered transportation in 1801 by ascending Camborne Hill.

Some interesting places to visit in Cornwall

The Tin Coast, from Cape Cornwall to Pendeen Watch. A place where fortunes were made and lost in the pursuit of winning Tin and Copper from under the ground and the sea. Wander the cliffs at Cape Cornwall and Botallack or see the magnificent winding engine still working at Levant.

Lose yourself in the mysterious world of The Lost Gardens where an exotic sub-tropical Jungle, atmospheric Victorian Pleasure Grounds, interactive Wildlife Project and the finest Productive Gardens in Britain all await your discovery. www.heligan.com

Beautiful family-run conservation park specialising in rare and unusual birds. Opportunities to get close to wildlife plus big indoor play centre. Home to 'World Parrot Trust' and 'Operation Chough'. www.paradisepark.org.uk.

Visit Wheal Martyn, set in a Victorian clay works, discover working waterwheels and modern china clay mining in action, explore nature trails and woodland walks, enjoy children's play and much more! www.wheal-martyn.com

Come and visit Geevor the largest preserved mine site in the country, the key centre within the Cornish Mining World Heritage Site! Interactive displays, exhibitions, underground tours and much more. www.geevor.com

Enjoy a ride from historic Launceston through the unspoilt Kensey Valley to the hamlet of Newmills. Our trains are hauled by Victorian steam locomotives which once worked in the slate mines of north Wales. More information at www.launcestonsr.co.uk

Visit our family run Farmshop selling Cornish wines, gins, breads, chocolates, cheeses, homemade pasta, plus home reared, free-range beef, lamb and pork from our award winning butchers. www.padstowfarmshop.co.uk

Come for a free visit to our Organic working Farm on the Lizard Peninsula. Meet the animals, stroll around the meadows, enjoy the tranquility by the ponds and of course, sample Roskilly's award winning ice cream! www.roskillys.co.uk